J 741.594 Caz
Cazenove, 1969-
The sisters. 2, Doing it our way /
$9.99   ocn961268172

WITHDRAWN

3 4028 10039 7174
HARRIS COUNTY PUBLIC LIBRARY

D0118187

Presented to
**Clear Lake City - County Freeman
Branch Library**

By

Friends of the Freeman Library

Harris County
Public Library
your pathway to knowledge

PAPERCUT𝖹

MORE GREAT GRAPHIC NOVEL SERIES AVAILABLE FROM PAPERCUTZ

THE SMURFS #21

MINNIE & DAISY #1

DISNEY FAIRIES #18

THE GARFIELD SHOW #6

BARBIE #1

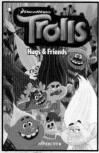

TROLLS #1

GERONIMO STILTON #17

THEA STILTON #6

FUZZY BASEBALL

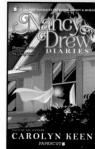

NANCY DREW DIARIES #

THE LUNCH WITCH #1

SCARLETT

ANNE OF GREEN BAGELS #1

THE RED SHOES

THE SISTERS #1

THE SMURFS, MINNIE & DAISY, DISNEY FAIRIES, THE GARFIELD SHOW, BARBIE and TROLLS graphic novels are available for $7.99 in paperback, and $12.99 in hardcover. GERONIMO STILTON and THEA STILTON graphic novels are available for $9.99 in hardcover only. FUZZY BASEBALL and NANCY DREW DIARIES graphic novels are available for $9.99 in paperback only. THE LUNCH WITCH, SCARLETT, and ANNE OF GREEN BAGELS graphic novels are available fo $14.99 in paperback only. THE RED SHOES graphic novel is available for $12.99 in hardcover only. Available from booksellers everywhere. You can also order online from www.papercutz.com. Or call 1-800-886-1223, Monday through Friday, 9–5 EST. MC, Visa, and AmEx accepted. To order by mail, please add $4.00 for postage and handling for first book ordered, $1.00 for each additional book and make check payable to NBM Publishing. Send to: Papercutz, 160 Broadway, Suite 700, East Wing, New York, NY 10038.

THE SMURFS, THE GARFIELD SHOW, BARBIE, TROLLS, GERONIMO STILTON, THEA STILTON, FUZZY BASEBALL, THE LUNCH WITCH, NANCY DREW DIARIES, THE RED SHOES, ANNE OF GREEN BAGELS, and SCARLETT graphic novels are also available wherever e-books are sold.

BARBIE ©2016 Mattel; DREAMWORKS TROLLS © 2016 DreamWorks Animation LLC. All Rights Reserved; LUNCH WITCH © 2016 Deb Lucke; DISNEY FAIRIES, DISNEY GRAPHIC NOVELS, MINNIE & DAISY; © 2016 Disney Enterprises, Inc.; GERONIMO STILTON and THEA STILTON; © 2016 Atlantyca S.p.A.; SCARLETT © Bayard Editions, 2013; THE RED SHOES © 2015 Metaphrog; FUZZY BASEBALL © 2016 by John Steven Gurney; ANNE OF GREEN BAGELS © 2016 by Jon Buller and Susan Schade; "THE GARFIELD SHOW" series © 2016 Dargaud Media. All rights reserved. © Paws. "Garfield" & Garfield characters TM & © Paws Inc. NANCY DREW DIARIES © 2016 by Simon & Schuster, Inc.

© Peyo - 2016 - Licensed through Lafig Belgium - www.smurf.com

2: "Doing It Our Way"

Art and colors
William

Story
Cazenove & William

PAPERCUTZ

New York

To my brothers: Alex, Franck, David, and Christopher.
To Christophe, who continues to astonish me.
To Olivier, for his faith in me, and for being available.

Thank you, Anelor, for your research. You guided me through hell!

Thank you, Marine, "Maureen," for not going all out on the originals with your glitter markers, and thank you for your help, Wendy, for putting the last pages in color.

—William

THE SISTERS #2 "Doing it Our Way"
Les Sisters [The Sisters] by Cazenove and William
© 2009 Bamboo Édition
Sisters, characters and related indicia are copyright, trademark and exclusive license of Bamboo Édition. English translation and all other editorial material © 2016 by Papercutz.
All rights reserved.

Story by Christophe Cazenove and William Maury
Art and color by William
Cover by William
Translation by Anne & Owen Smith
Lettering by Wilson Ramos Jr.
Special thanks to JayJay Jackson

No part of this book may be stored, reproduced or transmitted in Any form or by any means, electronic or mechanical, including photocopying, recording, or by any information storage and retrieval system, without written permission from the copyright holder.
For information address Bamboo Édition – 116, rue des Jonchères – BP 3, 71012 CHARNAY-lès-MÂCON cedex FRANCE
bamboo@bamboo.fr – www.bamboo.fr

Papercutz books may be purchased for business or promotional use. For information on bulk purchases please contact Macmilan Corporate and Premium Sales Department at (800) 221-7945 x5442

Production – Dawn Guzzo
Editorial Intern – Emelyne Tan
Editor – Jeff Whitman
Jim Salicrup
Editor-in-Chief

PB ISBN: 978-1-62991-595-1
HC ISBN: 978-1-62991-594-4

Printed in China
November 2016 by O.G. Printing Productions, LTD.
Units 2 & 3, 5/F, Lemmi Centre
50 Hoi Yuen Road
Kwon Tong, Kowloon

Distributed by Macmillan
First Papercutz Printing

WENDY! MAUREEN! TIME TO CLEAN YOUR ROOMS!

WHEN THE MOVIE'S OVER, MOM!

IT'S AT THE GOOD PART.

OH, NO, WENDY! IT JUST ENDED.

NO WORRIES! I'LL HIT "PLAY" AGAIN.

THE DANCING IS TO DIE FOR!

I THINK THIS IS MY FAVORITE MOVIE EVER!

GO BACK! I WANT TO SEE THAT GIRL DO A FLIP AGAIN!

THERE YOU GO!

LOOK AT THAT! SHE IS SO COOL. HIT IT AGAIN!

AGAIN! AGAIN! AGAIN!

OKAY! OKAY! OKAY!

CLICK CLICK CLICK

CLICK CLICK CLICK CLICK CLICK

GIRLS! YOUR ROOMS, NOW!

OKAY, OKAY! YOU DON'T HAVE TO TELL US 1000 TIMES!

IT'S SO ANNOYING TO HEAR THE SAME THING OVER AND OVER!

CAZENOVE & WILLIAM

5

TA-DAAAA!

WOW!

YOU'RE FANTASTIC WITH DOUGH WENDY!

AMAZING!

TOO TRUE, LOUISE.

TO GET THIS GOOD TAKES PAINSTAKING ATTENTION TO DETAIL.

PAIN STAKING?

LIKE VAMPIRES?

SEE? I USED MATCHSTICKS TO ATTACH THE GOBLIN'S ANTENNAE...

WOW!

AND TO FORM HIS EARS.

I KNOW BETTER THAN TO PLAY WITH MATCHES.

I MADE A BASE FOR HIM TO STAND ON.

SO HE WON'T GET AWAY?

THERE!

ONCE HE'S BAKED, YOU JUST POSE HIM WITH THE OTHERS.

LOOK, THERE'S DARTH VADER!

AND HOBBES-- HE'S SO CUTE!

YOU'RE SO LUCKY TO HAVE A SISTER LIKE WENDY!

YEAH, I KNOW!...

SHE LETS US GET AWAY WITH EVERYTHING.

~NOM~ ~NOM~

CRUNCH

CAZENOVE & WILLIAM

6

MY SISTER, MAUREEN, IS SUCH A HOOT!

SHE GETS EVERYTHING MIXED UP.

HA! DO TELL!

PING TWEET

"THE OTHER DAY, SHE REALLY CRACKED ME UP...

THE DENTIST SAID I NEED A FILLING-- BUT I'M ALREADY...

STUFFED!

"ONE TIME, DAD WAS REPAIRING A LEAKY FAUCET...

HERE, DADDY! IT WORKS GREAT ON MY DOLLY!

YOU DESERVE A BREAK TODAY!

AND SO I MADE A CAKE TODAY!

"SHE EVEN MADE A CAKE TO CHEER UP THE CAR WHEN IT NEEDED BRAKES...

"THE BEST WAS WHEN SHE SPRAYED HERSELF WITH INSECTICIDE 'CAUSE SHE HAD 'ANTS IN HER PANTS'!"

HAH!

HEY, WENDY!... MOM AND DAD WANT TO SEE YOU.

WHAT DO THEY WANT NOW?

THEY'RE GOING TO GIVE YOU A NEW VIDEO GAME, BECAUSE YOUR GRADES ARE SO GOOD.

AWESOME!

GAK!

OR MAYBE THEY'RE TAKING THE OLD ONE AWAY 'CAUSE HER GRADES ARE SO BAD...

...I GET EVERYTHING MIXED UP.

CAZENOVE & WILLIAM

WOW, THESE BIRDS ARE HUNGRY.

THEY EAT LIKE HORSES!

THEY'VE PIGGED OUT ON ALL THE BREAD CRUMBS.

THEY'RE *RAVENOUS!*

RAVENS OR NOT, THEY SCARFED ALL MY FAVORITE COOKIES.

NOT COOL!

IT'S LIKE THEY HAVEN'T EATEN FOR DAYS...

AND WE'RE OUT OF FOOD FOR THEM!

WAIT! I HAVE AN IDEA!

AHA! OUR LUNCHES! GENIUS IDEA!

I'M SURE THEY'LL LOVE IT!

HUH?

WE COULD'VE USED SOME HELP!

YOU *KNOW* WE HATE BOILED VEGETABLES!

WAAH...! NO MORE DESSERT FOR YOU!

CAZENOVE & WILLIAM

CAZENOVE & WILLIAM

WELL, THE TEACHER HAD US TURN TO PAGE 345 AND SHE MADE LULU READ THE WHOLE CHAPTER OUT LOUD... ONLY, HER CAT WAS UBER SICK THE NIGHT BEFORE AND THAT'S WHY SHE HADN'T SLEPT AND THAT'S WHY SHE ASKED SALLY AND EILEEN AND CHLOE AND MARGIE--OH, AND ME, OF COURSE--TO HELP HER STUDY--YOU KNOW, GIRL POWER... AFTER THAT, LEXI AND LAURA TALKED ABOUT THEIR VACATION IN THE MOUNTAINS...IT SOUNDED AWESOME...NEXT WEEK I GET TO WALK DARWIN--HE'S **SO ADORBS** WITH THOSE POINTY LITTLE EARS--HE'S A YOU'RE-SURE-TERROR-- I JUST LOVE THAT DOGGIE SO MUCH...WE GET FRIES AT LUNCH TODAY, YUM YUM YUM...DADDY'S GOING TO TEACH ME HOW TO DRAW A PANDA--DO YOU THINK PANDAS WEAR HELMETS? NAW, THAT'D BE TOO SILLY...

SO, DID YOUR PARENTS BUY YOU AN iPHONE?

NO--THEY COMPLAIN THERE'S TOO MUCH NOISE ALREADY.

CAZENOVE & WILLIAM

CAZENOVE & WILLIAM

YAY! WE'RE GOING TO HAVE OUR VERY OWN CLUBHOUSE!

WITH A FIREPLACE AND LOTS OF WINDOW !

CALM DOWN AND GIVE ME A HAND!

WHAT'S THIS FOR?

WHAT DO YOU *THINK*--A HAT?

IT'S FOR THE FLOOR. SHEESH. YOU GOING TO HELP ME OR NOT?

WHY ARE YOU MAKING THE FLOOR FIRST?

⇥GRUMBLE⇤
⇥GRUMBLE⇤
⇥GRUMBLE⇤

THAT'S STUPID!

WE SHOULD MAKE THE DOOR FIRST!

OH, YEAH?

WHEN YOU OPEN THE DOOR, WHERE DO YOU STEP?

I BET YOU'VE NEVER PUT A HOUSE TOGETHER.

NO, BUT I CAN TAKE *YOU* APART!

KRA KO OOO OOO M

WE SHOULD BUILD THE ROOF FIRST--IT'S ONLY LOGICAL!

FOR SURE!

CAZENOVE & WILLIAM

CAZENOVE & WILLIAM

QUICK! COME SEE!

DADDY'S DOING THE TECHNO-BOOGIE!

SLAP

YOU'RE NUTS! DAD DOESN'T EVEN *KNOW* HOW TO BOOGIE!

I SWEAR! CROSS MY HEART AND HOPE TO DIE!

HE BURSTS OUT LAUGHING WHEN HE SEES US DANCE.

MAYBE WE INSPIRED HIM.

HEE HEE!

OUR FRIENDS'LL BE SO JEALOUS WHEN THEY FIND OUT!

IF IT'S TRUE, WE HAVE TO POST A VIDEO FOR MY BLOG.

COME ON! HE'S IN HIS OFFICE!

HEAR THAT RACKET? HE MUST BE STILL DOING IT!

I JUST CAN'T WRAP MY MIND AROUND IT.

I DON'T KNOW-- HE JUST STARTED DANCING ...

...RIGHT AFTER HE DRANK THE COFFEE I FIXED HIM!

IT *IS* 7 SPOONFULS PER CUP, RIGHT?

OF COURSE! I BET HE'LL BE DANCING ALL NIGHT!

CAZENOVE & WILLIAM

WENDY...*WAIT!*

MR. BUN BUN GOT STUCK ON YOUR BACKPACK.

WELL, I DIDN'T DO IT ON PURPOSE.

YOU'RE BARKING MAD-- YOU'D MAKE A GREAT POLICE DOG!

YOU KNOW, IF THE BURGLARS STOLE A STUFFED ANIMAL, I COULD HELP YOU FIND IT!

CAZENOVE & WILLIAM

"AT FIRST, SUMMER CAMP WASN'T TOO GREAT.

WHY ARE THEY DRIVING AWAY?

DID WE DO SOMETHING BAD?

OF COURSE NOT! THIS PLACE IS GOING TO ROCK!

YEAH. SURE IT WILL.

"WE WERE OUT IN THE MIDDLE OF NOWHERE...

WHY SO GLUM?

WE'RE IN THE GREAT OUTDOORS!

IT SMELLS AWFULLY INDOORS TO ME.

MOUNTAIN BIKING! ARCHERY! ROCK CLIMBING! LAND ART!

DID YOU SEE THIS?!

=PFFT!= THEY DON'T EVEN HAVE HIP HOP. I WANT TO GO HOME.

C'MON! IT'S GOING TO BE FUN!

I WANT TO GO HOME!

HELLO, CHILDREN!

MY NAME IS BONITA...

...BUT YOU CAN CALL ME "BUN BUN."

WE'RE GOING TO HAVE A LOT OF FUN TOGETHER!

BUN BUN! THINGS ARE BETTER ALREADY!

CAZENOVE & WILLIAM

TODAY, CAMPERS, WE'RE GOING TO MAKE *LAND ART*!

WHAT'S *LAND ART*, BUN BUN?

IT'S A STUPID NAME FOR A STUPID GAME.

I WANT TO KNOW WHEN WE GET TO GO HOME.

STOP! PRETEND YOU DON'T KNOW ME.

YOU MAKE *LAND ART* BY DRAWING A HUGE PICTURE ON THE GROUND WITH NATURAL OBJECTS LIKE STONES OR PIECES OF WOOD...

CAN WE ERASE?

...YOUR PICTURE WILL BE VISIBLE FROM THE SKY.

WHAT CAN WE DRAW?

ANYTHING YOU WANT!

I'M GLAD TO SEE HER JOINING IN FOR ONCE...

⸮PUFF⸮ ⸮PUFF⸮

SHE SAID SHE DIDN'T WANT TO LEAVE...

CAZENOVE & WILLIAM

LOOK, CHILDREN!

A DOE WITH HER FAWN...

EVER SEEN ONE BEFORE?

YEP! IN "BAMBI"!

MR. GUIDE! WHAT'S THIS RED AND WHITE THINGIE?

IT'S NOT A *SMURF* HOUSE, IS IT?

SHEE HEE!

SNORT

I LOVE FLOWERS

OOH! MR. GUIDE! I SAW ONE OF THESE IN...

"ALICE IN WONDERLAND"!

I LOVE FLOWERS

MWA HA HA

LOL

GRRR

WOW! LOOK AT THESE BUGS...

I SAW SOME OF THEM IN...

"ANTZ"!

GRUMBLE GRUMBLE

JUST OUR LUCK, *HIS* FAVORITE MOVIE IS "CINDERELLA"!

SO LAME!

CAZENOVE & WILLIAM

CAZENOVE & WILLIAM

WHAT KIND OF FLOWER IS THIS?

A MORNING GLORY!

DO YOU KNOW ANY OTHER FUNNY FLOWER NAMES?

WELL, THERE ARE SNAPDRAGONS OVER THERE.

AND LOTS MORE!

LOOK, A LADY'S-SLIPPER!

THEY SHOULD COME IN PAIRS!

THESE ARE CALLED SNOWBALLS!

THEY'RE NOT EVEN COLD!

HERE'S A MEADOW FOXTAIL.

WILL I GET FLEAS IF I TOUCH IT?

HEY! THERE'S A WALLFLOWER OVER HERE!

⇒SNIFF⇐ ⇒SNIFF⇐ EWW, YUCK!

AND THAT'S A COW PIE!

STRANGE NAME--IT WOULDN'T TASTE VERY GOOD!

CAZENOVE & WILLIAM

24

HEY, AUDREY, HOW'S YOUR BIO PROJECT GOING?

GREAT! I PICKED "ANIMAL NUTRITION"...

...SO I WROTE DOWN ALL THE INGREDIENTS IN MY CAT'S KITTY KIBBLE.

HAHA!

AS LONG AS YOU DON'T HAVE TO TASTE IT!

I SHOULD'VE PICKED "ANIMAL BABIES," LIKE MEG-- MY DOG JUST HAD A LITTER OF PUPPIES!

SO CUTE!

MAIN STREET

SAMMIE'S GOT A COOL TOPIC, TOO: "HOW ANIMALS HUNT."

MY CAT WOULD BE GOOD FOR THAT, TOO.

WHAT'S YOUR TOPIC?

I PICKED "THE WILD ANIMAL IN ITS HABITAT."

WHOA! WON'T THAT BE TOO HARD?

NAH, NO PROBLEM. THE TRICK IS NOT TO GET SPOTTED.

Chapter 7:

The sister has a whole ritual for her mid-afternoon snack.

NYOM
CRUNCH
CHOMP

CAZENOVE & WILLIAM

25

CAZENOVE & WILLIAM

CAZENOVE & WILLIAM

IT'S NOT HERE EITHER...

A CLUBHOUSE CAN'T JUST DISAPPEAR!

ARE WE EVEN IN THE RIGHT FOREST?

I THINK WE SHOULD TURN AT THAT BIG OAK TREE.

YOU JUST SAID THAT.

DOESN'T THAT ROCK TELL YOU SOMETHING?

DON'T BE SILLY! ROCKS DON'T TALK.

WE'RE *NEVER* GOING TO FIND OUR CLUBHOUSE...

STOP! I CAN'T HEAR MYSELF THINK.

HERE IT IS! IT WAS PLAYING HIDE 'N' SEEK.

MY SECRET HIDEOUT!

I THOUGHT YOU WERE LOST FOREVER.

THERE'S GOT TO BE AN EASIER WAY TO FIND IT.

NOW WE'LL ALWAYS KNOW THE WAY!

SO MUCH FOR KEEPING IT SECRET!

CAZENOVE & WILLIAM

CAZENOVE & WILLIAM

SCORE!

WHAT DID YOU EXPECT?!

HOW COME WE RECYCLE STUFF?

IT'S TO GIVE THINGS A SECOND LIFE.

NOWADAYS THEY CAN TURN OLD SHAMPOO BOTTLES INTO ARMCHAIRS.

A SHAMPOO ARMCHAIR-- I LOVE IT!

"THEY CAN ALSO RECYCLE PLASTIC BOTTLES INTO SHIRTS AND PANTS--EVEN STUFFED ANIMALS!"

"THEY CAN TURN SODA CANS INTO CARS!"

VROOM

Cola

BOOM CHICKA!

BOOM CHICKA!

BOOM CHICKA!

HEY, WATCH OUT! IF YOU KEEP SHAKING IT--

-- IT'LL EXPLODE IN YOUR FACE!

CAZENOVE & WILLIAM

LOOK--! A BABY SEAL IN DANGER!

I'M ON IT!

JUST IN TIME!

IT'S NOT NICE TO HURT ANIMALS!

OW! OW! OW! POW BIFF BAM

DO YOU ENJOY BUILDING TRAPS FOR RHINOS?!

I PROMISE-- NEVER AGAIN!

NO WAY! LEAVE THOSE BUNNIES ALONE!

CRONK

MISSION ACCOMPLISHED!

DON'T WORRY... ANIMALS HAVE NOTHING TO FEAR FROM US.

RIGHT, WENDY?

YOU BET!

MY SISTER HAS GONE OVER TO THE DARK SIDE!

DIE! DIE! DIE!

STOMP STOMP STOMP

CAZENOVE x WILLIAM

31

CAZENOVE & WILLIAM

HURRY UP, LULU! WENDY'LL BE BACK SOON.

SHE MUST HAVE A PHOTO OF HER LATEST CRUSH SOMEWHERE.

UM, OKAY...

WATCH OUT! DON'T TOUCH THE SLIPPERS...

IT'S A TRAP!

BOOBY-TRAPPED SLIPPERS?!

YOUR SISTER'S ROOM IS A FORTRESS!

THEY'RE ALWAYS IN THE SAME PLACE. IF THEY'RE OFF BY A WHISKER, SHE'LL SPOT IT.

NO PHOTO UNDER HERE.

NOTHING IN THE CLOSET.

NOT HERE!

NOT HERE!

NOT HERE!

GOT IT!

WE CAN GO NOW.

CAREFUL! THE SLIPPERS!

OOPS!

-WNEW..

HA HA! WENDY WILL NEVER KNOW WE RAIDED HER ROOM.

LOL!

SHE NEEDS A NEW TRAP!

CAZENOVE & WILLIAM

HI-YAAAH!

WHOOMPH

HA HA! RIGHT IN THE FACE!

THWOMP

≈MMRF!≈

OKAY, SHRIMP--GIVE UP?!

IN YOUR DREAMS!

GIRLS!...IT'S TIME!

IF I COULD USE A PILLOW... I'D BE A BLACK BELT!

CAZENOVE & WILLIAM

WHENEVER MY SISTER LEARNS A NEW WORD, SHE USES IT ALL THE TIME...

BUT NEVER CORRECTLY!

YUM!... BREAD AND *SCRAM!*

BRRR...THE WATER'S SO *SCRAMMY!*

TODAY WE STUDIED *SCRAMMING.*

MY TURN TO *SCRAM* THE DISHES!

CRASH CRACK

I GOTTA *SCRAM!*

HA! SHE FINALLY USED IT RIGHT.

CAZENOVE & WILLIAM

HURRY UP, MAUREEN!

I'M COMING!

WE'RE GOING TO BE LATE TO THE DENTIST.

I CAN'T FIND MY OTHER SHOE!

AGAIN?!

HAVE YOU LOOKED UNDER YOUR BED YET?

NO-- I NEVER PUT THEM THERE!

NOPE!

WHERE'S IT HIDING?

UH-UH.

SOOOO?

I DON'T GET IT...

WENDY MUST'VE HIDDEN IT.

C'MON, GET IN THE CAR.

WE'LL BUY YOU A NEW PAIR ON THE WAY TO THE DENTIST.

Oof!

HURRRRY...

YOU DIDN'T REALLY THINK YOUR MOM WOULD FORGET TO TAKE YOU TO THE DENTIST AFTER BUYING YOU SHOES, DID YOU?

COULDN'T HURT!

CAZENOVE & WILLIAM

36

HI-YAAAH!

SPLAT

FRIP

SO, GIRLS, WHAT SPORT WOULD YOU LIKE TO SIGN UP FOR THIS YEAR?

FASHION DESIGN!

CAZENOVE x WILLIAM

CAZENOVE & WILLIAM

38

SISTERS CAN BE SO GULLIBLE...

MAUREEN BELIEVES EVERYTHING I SAY.

Y'KNOW, ON THE OTHER SIDE OF THE PLANET, RAIN FALLS *UP.*

FOR REAL?

PLITCH

IF A HEN EATS DICE, SHE LAYS SQUARE EGGS.

Cluck

SRSLY?

AND OF COURSE, CHOCOLATE MILK COMES FROM BROWN COWS.

REALLY?

I BET MASEY-WASEY TOLD YOU ALL THOSE THINGS.

WHADDAYA MEAN?

I READ IN YOUR DIARY THAT HE TELLS YOU *LOTS* OF STORIES.

BUT THERE WERE SOME WORDS I COULDN'T UNDERSTAND, SO I GAVE IT TO MOM.

MOM! STOP! DON'T LOOOOOK!

SISTERS CAN BE SO GULLIBLE... WENDY BELIEVES EVERYTHING I SAY.

CAZENOVE & WILLIAM

CAN YOU SPREAD SOME OF THIS CREAM ON MY FACE?

WHAT'S IT FOR?

IT'S A SKIN CLEANSER.

AND IT GETS RID OF INFECTIOUS AGENTS!

SNIFF
SNIFF

IT REALLY WORKS!

SMELLS LIKE FLOWERS.

AREN'T YOU WORRIED IT WILL *ATTRACT* INSECTY AGENTS?

LOL!

IT'S BEAUTY TIME!

C'MON ALREADY! WHAT'S TAKING YOU SO LONG?

SINCE YOU'RE IN SUCH A HURRY...

HEY!

SPLISH SPLOSH

HERE YOU GO!

EWW! WHAT'S THAT HORRIBLE STENCH?!

THIS ISN'T MY CREAM!

NAH! IT'S DADDY'S STINKY CHEESE...

IF YOU WANT TO GET RID OF INSECTS...

YOU NEED SOMETHING STINKY!

GAH!

AAAAAAAAAAAAAHHH...

AND IT GETS RID OF BIG SISTERS!

IT REALLY WORKS!

CAZENOVE & WILLIAM

IT'S SUNDAY!

ON SUNDAY, WE HELP DAD WITH YARD WORK.

SO MUCH FUN!

I'LL GET THE MOWER. YOU'RE TOO LITTLE.

FINE. BE THAT WAY.

I'LL GET THE BIG FAN!

THAT'S A "RAKE," SILLY.

SHEARS, EXTRA-LARGE TRASH BAGS...

CLASSY GARDENING GLOVES!

GREAT!

CLAP

DADDDDDY!

DAD WILL BE SO GLAD WE SET OUT THE TOOLS FOR HIM.

WE'RE SUCH A BIG HELP.

CAZENOVE & WILLIAM

SNOW WHITE SANG AS SHE CLEANED HOUSE...

THE BIRDS SANG ALONG...

...AND HELPED...HER...CLEAN...

HELLO, MY PRETTY...

...HOME ALONE?

WELL, YEAH. THE DWARVES ARE OUT HUNTING FOR BLING.

CARE FOR AN APPLE?

HMMM... I WAS GOING TO MAKE A PB&J.

NOT VERY ORGANIC!

C'MON, DON'T BE SHY.

I'LL CUT IT IN HALF.

WELL, OKAY THEN.

IT'S REALLY GOOD!

THAT'S WHAT YOU THINK.

BWA HA HA HA

≶ICK≶

≶CHOMP≶

BWA HA HA HA HA HA HA HA HA HA HA HA HA

≶UKK≶

≶BK≶

≶CHOKE≶

≶AKK≶

MAUREEN! TIME FOR YOUR MEDICINE!

DON'T BE SUCH A BABY. I CUT IT IN HALF SO IT'S EASIER TO SWALLOW.

NO! YOU CAN'T TRICK ME AGAIN!

≶MMM≶ SMELLS LIKE APPLE!

CAZENOVE & WILLIAM

WE'RE SELLING RAFFLE TICKETS FOR OUR SCHOOL.

WANT SOME?

BUY MY TICKETS!

YEAH! LOTS OF STUFF TO WIN. HUGE PRIZES.

C'MON-- IT'S WORTH A SHOT.

A DVD PLAYER, VIDEO GAMES, MP3 PLAYERS...

HAND-PAINTED EGGS...

IF YOU DON'T BUY ANY, YOU'LL HAVE NO CHANCE TO WIN.

WE DON'T TAKE MONOPOLY MONEY!

HEY, LOOK! OVER THERE!

WHO IS THAT GUY?

WE NEED TO SET HIM STRAIGHT.

=MMMPH.=

YOU CAN'T JUST *GIVE* TICKETS *AWAY!*

THIS IS OUR TERRITORY, MISTER! *BUZZ OFF!*

CAZENOVE & WILLIAM

43

CAZENOVE & WILLIAM

"ONCE UPON A TIME, IN A MAGICAL LAND...

...THERE LIVED A GORGEOUS PRINCESS IN A GRAND CASTLE..."

WAIT--! IS THIS THE ONE WHERE THE WITCH SETS A TRAP WITH PEARS OR SOMETHING?!

NOT THAT ONE!

IS IT THE ONE WITH THE PRINCE WHO FIGHTS THE DRAGON?!

I'M THE ONE READING THE STORY, OKAY?!

YOU'RE NOT HELPING ME FALL ASLEEP, YOU KNOW!

I BET IT'S THE ONE WITH THE GREEN GOBBLE-UNS!

CENTER-ELLA?

THE TOAD PRINCE?

SEVEN-LEAK BOOTS?

JACK AND THE BEANS TALK?

CHOMP

GRRRRR

I DUNNO... THE ONE WITH...ME?!

CAN'T FALL ASLEEP?

NAH! WENDY'S NO GOOD AT TELLING STORIES!

CAZENOVE & WILLIAM

LET'S CHECK OUT THAT NEW DANCE VIDEO!

JUST A SEC. I'LL GET RID OF THE *BRAT!*

HEY, WANT TO GO ON A SCAVENGER HUNT?

I DON'T KNOW--WHAT IS IT?

YOU FOLLOW CLUES TO FIND A SURPRISE.

YOU'RE GOING TO LOVE IT.

A...VIEW... FROM...YOUR...FEET... TO...WHERE...YOU... EAT!

YAY! I FOUND THE FIRST CLUE!

TURN... OVER...THE... GNOME...IN... HIS...GARDEN HOME.

COOL! IT'S WORKING!

AT...THE... BIG...FRONT... DOOR, YOU'LL... LEARN...SOME... MORE.

HA! MY PLAN CAN'T FAIL.

NOW WE CAN WATCH--

WHERE'S THE NEXT CLUE?

OVER THAT WAY.

I *LOVE* SCAVENGER HUNTS!

...

CAZENOVE & WILLIAM

WENDY! GET YOUR REAR IN GEAR!

WHAT'S UP?

WHY THE RUSH?

THE GENERAL WANTS TO SEE US.

W AND M, THE WORLD IS IN GRAVE DANGER, NOW MORE THAN EVER...

WE NEED YOU!

YOU CAN COUNT ON US, SIR!

WICKED COOL!

WE HAVEN'T WORN THESE SINCE...WHEN?

≶UNH!≶

SINCE WE THRASHED THE TROLLS WHO WRECKED OUR CLUBHOUSE.

≶ARGH!≶ IT'S TOO...

TOO TIGHT!

TOO SILLY!

WHAT DO YOU MEAN, THEY'RE TOO SMALL?

THEY WILL BE... SOMEDAY.

HEE HEE

CAZENOVE & WILLIAM

48

HEY...WHY ARE *YOU* UP SO EARLY?

DID YOU HAVE A NIGHTMARE?

DID YOU FALL OUT OF BED?

WHY LEAVE A NICE WARM BED WHEN YOU DON'T HAVE TO?!

I LIKE TO WATCH YOU RUSH OFF TO SCHOOL BEFORE I GO BACK TO BED.

ENJOY YOUR CLASSES!

CAZENOVE & WILLIAM

WHEN WE FIGHT, WE DON'T HOLD BACK...

POOPY-HEAD!

ZIT-FACE!

SHUT YOUR FACE, BRAT!

BUT THE FIGHT NEVER LASTS LONG...

ONE OF US ALWAYS SENDS A NICE NOTE TO THE OTHER...

My pretty Maureen, please forgive me for calling you a nuisance

your sister who loves you.

I luv you my deer sister and I appolujize, Maureen

WHEN WE MAKE UP, WE DON'T HOLD BACK...

BOP

ARRRGGHH

BUT THE TRUCE NEVER LASTS LONG, EITHER...

I LUUURRVE YOU!

WELL, I LOVE YOU MORE!

I HATE YOUR GUTS!

LET ME GO, LAME-BRAIN!

CAZENOVE & WILLIAM

IT'S NOT FAIR!

I FEEL LIKE AN OLD RECYCLING BIN.

EVERYTHING I OWN IS A HAND-ME-DOWN FROM WENDY.

THIS THINGAMAJIG IS *ANCIENT*... WAY OUT OF STYLE!

EVEN MY SHOES ARE SECONDHAND... OR SECOND*FOOT!*

REALLY, DADDY, I'D LOOK BETTER IN *YOUR* OLD SLIPPERS!

I NEVER GET NEW BOOKS...

YOU USED UP ALL THE STORIES ALREADY!

PURPLE SMURFS

...LET ALONE TOYS.

BROKEN. NO BATTERIES. ALL BENT AND SCRATCHED.

SHEESH!

NOT TO MENTION CLOTHES.

TA-DA!

NO WAY! DON'T YOU DARE BUY THAT OUTFIT...

I REFUSE TO WEAR IT!

CAZENOVE & WILLIAM

YAY!

GIRLS! NANA AND PAPA ARE HERE!

YAHOO!

WHEN OUR GRANDPARENTS GO ON VACATION, WE TAKE CARE OF THEIR ADORABLE DOGGIE.

DARWIN!

YIP!

YIP!

SOOOOO CUTE!

WE'LL TAKE SUPER GOOD CARE OF HIM.

DON'T WORRY ABOUT A THING!

LET'S HAVE A RACE!

TO THE GARDEN AND BACK!

YIP!

YIP!

YIP!

WHEEE! I'M GETTING DIZZY!

ARF! ARF!

I'M ON THE SPIN CYCLE!

A KILLER HIGH JUMP!

NEXT LET'S THROW SOME BALLS FOR DARWIN.

BLUE, BLUE!

GET MINE!

NO, MINE!

THE RED ONE!

JUMP HIGHER!

MISSED!

C'MON, DARWIN!

ARF!

ARF!

I KNOW YOU CAN DO IT!

UM... DARWIN HAS A PROBLEM.

HE'S ALL RUN DOWN.

DO YOU HAVE ANY NEW BATTERIES?

PANT PANT PANT PANT

CAZENOVE & WILLIAM

CAZENOVE & WILLIAM

CAZENOVE & WILLIAM

"WE DON'T NEED TO GO TO THE MOUNTAINS BECAUSE EVERY YEAR, THE SNOW COMES TO US...

WENDY...IT'S SNOWING!

"AS SOON AS THE FIRST SNOWFLAKES FALL, WE RUN AROUND LIKE CRAZY...

PLOP

"THEN WE CHOOSE A NICE SQUISHY TRASH BAG...

HEE HEE HEE

"AND WE HURTLE DOWN THE HILLSIDE AT FULL SPEED...

YEAH!

YIPPIEEE!

THIS IS TOTALLY BETTER THAN A MOUNTAIN!

WHAT A BLAST!

"WE HAVE THE SNOW ALL TO OURSELVES...

THIS IS THE LIFE!

"BUT JUST LIKE AT THE MOUNTAIN...

"IT'S A LONG WAY BACK TO THE TOP."

CAZENOVE & WILLIAM

GOT LOTS TO DO?

YEAH. TONS.

I'M GOING TO TRY AND GET A HEAD START.

ME TOO!

CAN YOU GET YOURS DONE?

NOT SURE. I MIGHT ASK MOM FOR HELP.

WAP

MAYBE WE COULD DO IT *TOGETHER.*

REALLY? YOU MEAN IT?

AWESOME!

I'LL GET THE MARKERS!

WE NEED TO GET GOING ON THESE CHRISTMAS WISH LISTS!

RIGHT! THERE'S NO TIME LIKE THE *PRESENT!*

CAZENOVE & WILLIAM

HEY, IT'S *MY* TURN TO USE THE COMPUTER!

TOO BAD!

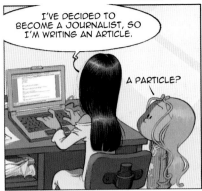

I'VE DECIDED TO BECOME A JOURNALIST, SO I'M WRITING AN ARTICLE.

A PARTICLE?

IT'S A PAPER THAT TELLS WHAT'S GOING ON IN THE WORLD.

THEN GET SOME PAPER AND LET ME USE THE COMPUTER!

"PAPER" IS JUST A WORD THAT WE JOURNALISTS USE, SILLY.

WHATEVS. HOW DO YOU FIND OUT WHAT'S GOING ON?

TAP TAP

TAP

YOU INVESTIGATE. WATCH TV, LISTEN TO THE RADIO, SURF THE NET...

BUT THAT'S WHAT YOU DO FOR FUN!

SOUNDS FISHY TO ME!

AH, NEVER MIND... YOU'RE TAKING ALL THE FUN OUT OF IT.

≡NYAH≡ ≡NYAH!≡

CLAP

WHAT'S BUGGING YOU, WENDY?

I'VE DECIDED TO GIVE UP JOURNALISM... TOO MUCH PRESSURE!

CAZENOVE & WILLIAM

53

C'MON! BACK FLIP!

SNAP

WOW, YOU'RE REALLY GOOD AT DOG-TRAINING, WENDY!

YOU'RE THE TIP! YOU'RE THE TOP! TEACH ME HOW! TEACH ME HOW!

OKAY! LOL!

TO GET HIM TO OBEY, YOU NEED TO MOTIVATE HIM WITH SOMETHING HE LIKES.

YEAH...MAKE HIM DO ANOTHER TRICK SO I CAN SEE.

SIT, DARWIN!

BOO-YAH! HE DID IT AGAIN!

I WANT A *MOTIVE* TOO!

HE OBEYS BECAUSE HE KNOWS HE'S GOING TO BE REWARDED.

YIP! YIP! YIP!

DID YOU TEACH HIM ANYTHING ELSE?

HE'S DOING GREAT.

YOU WANT TO SEE?

A CAROB CHIP COOKIE WILL BRING SUCCESS!

COOKIES

GUARANTEED!

ARF!

ARF!

CAZENOVE & WILLIAM

FETCH, DARWIN, FETCH!

YIP! YIP! YIP!

GOOD DOGGIE!

YIP!

GO FIND IT, BOY!

YIP! YIP!

MOM, DARWIN FINDS HIS TOY NO MATTER WHERE IT IS!

YES, SWEETIE. HE'S A GOOD DOGGIE!

HE'S VERY GOOD...UNLIKE **SOMEONE** I KNOW..

HEH HEH HEH

...WHO HID HER MATH TEST...

...'CAUSE SHE GOT A VERY VERY BAD GRADE!

A-HEM!

WHAT? IT'S THE TRUTH!

⁑HUMPH!⁑ WHEN YOU FIND THINGS, YOU'RE A GOOD DOGGIE! WHEN I FIND THINGS, I GET PUNISHED!

NOT FAIR!

CAZENOVE & WILLIAM

55

HEYYYY! I BET YOU HAVE A *HOT DATE* TONIGHT!

GRUMPH

IS MASEY-WASEY TAKING YOU OUT TO SEE A KISSY-FACE MOVIE? *MMWAH!* *MMWAH!*

NOPE. NOT EVEN CLOSE!

I BET YOU'RE GOING SHOE SHOPPING...

SO YOU NEED SPARKLY TOES.

BZZT! WRONG AGAIN!

SO WHY GET ALL PRETTY?

YOU'LL SEE.

WENDYY...MAUREEEN... GET DOWN HERE!

WE'RE COMING!

I WOULD *LOVE* TO LEND A HAND, BUT MY POLISH ISN'T DRY YET.

NOW I GET IT.

CAZENOVE & WILLIAM

CAN YOU DOUBLE CHECK TO MAKE SURE I HAVE EVERYTHING?

AGAIN...? WHAT A DRAG!

OKAY. LOCAL MAP...CHECK. BOTTLE OF WATER... CHECK. WHERE'S THE POWER BAR?

UM... I ATE IT.

STRESS.

LITTLE WHITE PEBBLES... GOT THEM.

IT'S IN MY PANTS POCKET.

BUN BUN... CHECK. CELL PHONE... NOT HERE.

RUMMAGE RUMMAGE

AND LOOK, I BROUGHT A COMPASS TOO.

GREAT! I CAN TELL DADDY TO STOP LOOKING FOR IT.

I STAPLED IT TO MY JACKET.

ALL SET! BE SURE TO LOOK FOR LANDMARKS SO YOU CAN FIND YOUR WAY BACK.

IF YOU'RE NOT BACK BY DINNERTIME, I'LL COME LOOKING FOR YOU.

DON'T TALK TO STRANGERS. IF YOU GET LOST...CALL.

BE BRAVE, MAUREEN. YOU CAN DO IT!

OKAY.

IS THIS THE FIRST TIME SHE'S GONE SHOPPING ALL BY HERSELF?

IS IT THAT OBVIOUS?

SUPERMARKET

CAZENOVE & WILLIAM

57

WENDY, WHAT'S THIS DOOHICKEY?

SOME WEIRD KIND OF CLOCK?

IT'S A BAROMETER, SILLY.

YEAH? WHAT KIND OF BAR DOES IT MEASURE... CHOCOLATE OR SOAP?

DON'T YOU KNOW ANYTHING?

A BAROMETER SHOWS WHEN THE WEATHER IS GOING TO CHANGE AND IF WE'RE GOING TO HAVE SUNSHINE OR A BAD STORM.

REALLY? IT SAYS ALL THAT?

IT'S LIKE A NEW KIND OF BAR CODE!

WHY IS IT HANGING UP OUTSIDE?

SO IT CAN BE CLOSER TO THE CLOUDS.

AWESOMESAUCE!

MAUREEN, ARE YOU SURE IT CAN GIVE US THE ANSWERS TO OUR SPELLING TEST?

OF COURSE-- HAVEN'T YOU HEARD OF A BAR EXAM?

CAZENOVE & WILLIAM

WAAAAAH...

DON'T WORRY, MR. BUN BUN. I'M ONLY PRACTICING MY DISAPPOINTED WAIL.

IT'S A VERY USEFUL SKILL.

IT WORKS ON MOM...

WOOT!

OKAY, YOU CAN STAY UP TILL THE SHOW IS OVER!

HMFF

...ON WENDY...

WAAAAAH...

OKAY! OKAY! YOU MAY BORROW MY GAME NINTENDOX.

...ON DADDY...

BOOKS

BUT ALL MY FRIENDS HAVE ONE! IF I DON'T GET ONE, THEY'LL THINK I'M STOOOOOPID!

ALL RIGHT, ALL RIGHT! GET THE BOOK.

...EVEN ON NAT...

OKAY, I'LL DO YOUR HOMEWORK FOR YOU.

I'M UNSTOPPABLE! NO ONE CAN RESIST ME.

PEANUT

WOHWOHWOH

?

HOW DOES HE DO IT?

HE ALWAYS GETS WHAT HE WANTS.

SNARK
CHOMP
SNARF

CAZENOVE & WILLIAM

OKAY, WENDY, I'LL LET YOU WALK *DARWIN* TODAY.

IT'S THE LEAST I CAN DO FOR MY DEAR SISTER.

NOOOO!

SNIP
SNIP
SNIP

CAN'T YOU SEE I'M REALLY BUSY?!

BUT IT'S SO MUCH FUN! YOU ALWAYS COMPLAIN THAT YOU NEVER GET TO WALK HIM.

I KNOW WHAT YOU'RE UP TO. YOU DON'T FOOL ME.

IT'S RAINING CATS AND DOGS OUTSIDE AND YOU DON'T WANT TO GET WET.

PRETTY PRETTY PLEASE, WENDY! I'LL BE THE *PERFECT* SISTER!

HEY— IT'S YOUR PROBLEM, NOT MINE!

I'M *DONE!*

PUH-LEEZE
PUH-LEEZE
PUH-LEEZE

BUT YOU KNOW WHAT HAPPENS WHEN DARWIN GOES OUT IN THE RAIN...

HE GETS ALL SOGGY AND STINKY.

ALL RIGHT, ALL RIGHT...NOW HE'S THE ONE WHO DOESN'T WANT TO GO OUT.

GRRR...

UNH!

BE A GOOD DOGGIE!

COME ON!... YOU HAVEN'T GONE PEEPEE SINCE THIS MORNING!

GRRRrrr...

NOOoo!

HA! WHEN IT RAINS, *YOU* GET ALL SOGGY AND STINKY, TOO!

CAZENOVE & WILLIAM

SUPER W, SUPER M-- I HAVE BAD NEWS... *THE BLOB* IS LOOSE..

AND I'M AFRAID HE HAS...

A BONE TO PICK WITH YOU!

LOL! I DIDN'T KNOW HE HAD ANY BONES!

SQUELTCH

?

GLOBBOOOGAHH!

⇒EWWW.⇐ I FORGOT HOW GROSS HE CAN BE.

ARE YOU A GLUTTON FOR PUNISHMENT?

HI-YAAH!

BLOB

YICK! MY NICE CLEAN COSTUME...

SPLOOTCH

DO SOMETHING, SUPER M...

ONCE IT'S GONE THIS FAR, THERE'S NO WAY TO STOP IT.

⇒ACK!⇐ I'VE BEEN SLIMED!

WATCH OUT, HE'S GOING TO BLOW!

OH, NO! NOT THAT...

I CAN'T BELIEVE HOW GROSS A DOG CAN BE.

FOR A PUREBRED, HE'S NOT SO PURE.

YUCK!

CAZENOVE & WILLIAM

61

LOOK, MAUREEN! YOU CAN SEE OUR HOUSE FROM HERE!

YOU CAN EVEN SEE OUR CLUBHOUSE.

HUH?

THIS PEBBLE IS SOOO CUTE!

LOOK AT IT!

YOU'RE NUTS!

IT'S SO ADORABLE WITH ITS LITTLE PINK AND BLUE SPECKS!

DON'T YOU THINK IT'S CUTE?

≶PFFT!≶ IT'S JUST A PIECE OF ROCK!

JUST LIKE MILLIONS OF OTHER ROCKS AROUND HERE.

BO-RING!

YOU JUST DON'T GET THE POETRY OF PEBBLES.

THE "POETRY OF PEBBLES"...

IT'S A GORGEOUS DAY IN THE MOUNTAINS, WITH FLOWERS, PARAGLIDERS, A SUPER VIEW, AND EVERYTHING...

AND SHE GETS ALL EXCITED ABOUT GRAVEL!

SOMETIMES I WONDER IF YOU'RE REALLY MY SISTER.

YOU'VE GOT ROCKS IN YOUR HEAD.

≶SIGH.≶

HEY, MOM, IF YOU'RE LOOKING FOR A PRESENT FOR WENDY...

FORGET ABOUT THIS STUFF...SHE HATES ROCKS.

CAZENOVE & WILLIAM

CAZENOVE & WILLIAM

I AM *SO DEAD!*

THERE'S A TEST THIS MORNING...I'M NO GOOD AT SPELLING...I'M NEVER GOING TO GET IT...

IF YOU WANT, I CAN HELP!

I KNOW SOME SIMPLE TRICKS TO HELP YOU REMEMBER HOW A WORD IS SPELLED.

AT THIS POINT, I NEED A MIRACLE.

TRUST ME... THEY'RE FOOL PROOF.

BUT I'M NOT A FOOL!

LOOK, WHEN YOU *APPEAR,* YOU'RE *POSITIVELY PRESENT,* RIGHT?

SO "APPEAR" HAS 2 P'S.

COOL! GOT ANY MORE?

IF YOU *PERCEIVE* WITH YOUR *EYE,* YOU *SEE...*

SO "PERCEIVE" HAS A C IN THE MIDDLE!

WHEN YOU *WHISTLE,* YOU *SOUND TOO LOUD...*

AND "WHISTLE" HAS AN S-T-L.

THANK *Y-O-U,* WENDY.

SO, MAUREEN, DO YOU KNOW HOW TO WRITE THEM OR NOT?

The teacher is a meenie!

Fill in the blanks: A ___ EAR
PER ___ VE
WHI ___ E

CAZENOVE & WILLIAM

65

THERE'S A *TON* OF SNOW!

WOW!

IT'S WONDER-FUL!

ARE YOU SURE? DIDN'T YOU LEAVE MR. BUN BUN IN THE YARD LAST NIGHT?

HUH?

MR. BUN BUN... OUTSIDE?

BUT...

HE SLEPT ON MY PILLOW... DIDN'T HE?

I'M SURE HE ATE DINNER WITH ME.

I HAD A NAPKIN IN ONE HAND, AND MR. BUN BUN IN THE OTHER.

RIGHT?

IF YOU SAY SO.

BESIDES, I *NEVER* LEAVE HIM OUTSIDE!

OF COURSE NOT.

ALMOST TOO SIMPLE.

LOL!

I WOULDN'T LEAVE MR. BUN BUN OUT IN THE COLD.

I'LL *PROVE* TO YOU HE'S NOT OUTSIDE.

DAD...CAN I WATCH TV NOW? THE FRONT WALK IS CLEARED.

WHERE ARE YOU?

‹SNORF›‹SNIFF›

CAZENOVE & WILLIAM

SO DID YOU LIKE THE MOVIE, MASON?

YEAH. I LOVED THE PART WITH THE VAMPIRES. YOU SCREAMED...

...AND HELD ME CLOSE FOR COMFORT.

WENDYYY... HELP ME FINISH MY SNOWMAN.

IT'S TOO BIG FOR ME.

⸗ARRGH!⸗ CAN'T YOU SEE I'M BUSY?!

COME QUICK, OR ELSE HE'LL FALL APART.

COME ON, OR I'LL TELL DADDY YOU WERE KISSING A BOY.

THE SUNSHINE IS GOING TO KILL HIM!

DO YOU WANT HIM TO DIE BEFORE HE'S DONE?

I COULDN'T CARE LESS ABOUT YOUR STUPID SNOWMAN. I'VE GOT BETTER THINGS TO DO.

THAT'S IT! YOU'RE NOT MY SISTER ANYMORE.

FINE! I'D LOVE TO BE AN ONLY CHILD.

SLAM

WHOOSH

?

THWUMP

OH, I SEE-- YOU WANTED TO MAKE YOUR OWN SNOWMAN!

⸗BLEFF!⸗

CAZENOVE & WILLIAM

67

OH, GOOD, YOU'RE HERE...UM... I WANTED TO SAY SOMETHING...

I'M...SORRY FOR BEING SUCH A HUGE PEST TODAY.

I'M SORRY I WRECKED YOUR SNOWMAN...

...AND TOLD DARWIN TO PEE ON IT.

AND I FEEL SO BAD FOR CUTTING UP YOUR MAGAZINES...

≶AARGH!≶

...RUINING YOUR FAVE SWEATER...

...SPOILING YOUR MAKEUP!

SORRY!

...BUSTING YOUR NINTENDOX...

...I PROMISE TO BEHAVE...

...FROM NOW ON!

OKAY, OKAY... I'M GOING TO LET YOU DO YOUR HOMEWORK IN PEACE...

THANKS FOR NOT YELLING AT ME...

...YOU'RE MY FAVORITE SISTER.

ALL SET!

NOW FOR THE NINTENDOX, THE FAVE SWEATER, AND ALL THE REST!

CAZENOVE & WILLIAM

EXCELLENT! ALL HE NEEDS ARE EYES AND STUFF.

BEEP BEEP! COMING THROUGH!

HERE WE GO! RIGHT OUT OF THE FRIDGE.

I GET TO PUT HIS NOSE ON!

HEY, OUR SNOWMAN'S EYES...HAVE EYES!

AND HE'S GOT CAULIFLOWER EARS!

THESE RADISHES GIVE HIM A RAKISH SMILE!

AND HE'S GOT HANDS AS COOL AS CUCUMBERS.

HA HA!

LOL

A STRING OF GARLIC FOR A NECKLACE.

STYLIN'! AND HE'S SAFE FROM...

VAMPIRES!

WHAT WERE YOU THINKING?! YOU COULD'VE ASKED. NOW HOW AM I SUPPOSED TO MAKE LUNCH?

LOST YOUR APPETITE, GIRLS?

OF COURSE! YOU'VE GOT TO UNDERSTAND, MOM--WE'RE NOT CANNIBALS!

CAZENOVE & WILLIAM

SAY, WHAT'D WE DO YESTERDAY?

WE RODE OUR SLEDS UNTIL YOU KNOCKED ME INTO THE FROZEN POND.

WHAT ABOUT FRIDAY?

WE STAYED INSIDE AND PLAYED BOARD GAMES.

ON THURSDAY WE WATCHED DVD'S...

ON WEDNESDAY WE MADE PANCAKES.

SO IT'S BEEN A REALLY LONG TIME SINCE...

YEAH, YOU'RE RIGHT.

YOU WENT INTO THE POND ON *PURPOSE!*

WHO WANTS TO SWIM IN WINTER?!

IT'S NOT *MY FAULT* YOU CAN'T STEER A SLED!

I SHOULD JUST--

BASH

HEY! MY SNOWMAN!

YOU'RE JUST *MEAN!*

STOP FIGHTING!

CAN'T YOU GET ALONG FOR FIVE MINUTES?

IF WE GO TOO LONG WITHOUT GETTING YELLED AT, MOM AND DAD'LL THINK WE DON'T LOVE EACH OTHER.

WE DO IT FOR THEM.

CAZENOVE & WILLIAM

WE'RE GOING TO **ATOMIZE** YOU!

WE ARE SUPER STRONG!

⇒PFFT!⇐... BETTER LEARN TO AIM FIRST.

WENDY, DUCK!

YOU COULDN'T HIT THE BROAD SIDE OF A B--

YAY! ANOTHER POINT FOR US!

SPLAT

IT'S 100 TO 101! WE'RE STILL AHEAD BY ONE.

SPLAT

ANOTHER DIRECT HIT.

SPLAT

102

101

SPLAT

102

YOU CAN'T EVEN COUNT!

SPLAT

IT'S HARD TO TELL WHO WON... WE'RE ALL COVERED IN SNOW.

WE WON BY A PONT!

AND THAT'S FINAL!

AAAAAAAH--CHOOOOO!

YOUR TEMP IS 102 AND MINE'S 101. YOU WIN BY A POINT!

YIPPEE.

SNIFF

SNIFFLE

CAZENOVE & WILLIAM

71

CAZENOVE & WILLIAM

GIRLS, TIME TO SET THE TABLE!

RATS!

FIRST, BRING EVERYTHING IN FROM OUTSIDE.

NOOOOooo...

DO WE HAVE TO BRING *EVERYTHING*?

YEP, EVERYTHING.

≶WHEW!≶ I'M STARVING!

WHERE'S MAUREEN?... DIDN'T SHE COME IN WITH YOU?

YEAH, YEAH...

D'OH!

SHE HASN'T QUITE BROUGHT *EVERYTHING* IN YET.

LOL!

CAZENOVE & WILLIAM

73

MONDAY

THREE WHOLE DAYS UNTIL IT COMES OUT.

I CAN HARDLY WAIT!

THIS IS TORTURE.

TUESDAY

TWO DAYS...

GREAT! NO PROBLEMS REPORTED WITH THE RELEASE.

The Tims

SPECIAL LIMITED EDITION

The Tims

WEDNESDAY

TOMORROW.

TOMORROW.

THE DAY

LOOK AT THE CROWD! THE GAME STORE MUST HAVE OPENED EARLY.

WE'LL HAVE A BETTER CHANCE IF WE SPLIT UP.

UM...HEY... JUST ONE TO A CUSTOMER...

NEW

The TiMS 4

THE TIMS!

GOT IT!

SWISH

YES!

The Tims

I CAN'T BELIEVE YOU GOT IT!

NOW WE'LL HAVE PEACE AND QUIET FOR AT LEAST TWO WEEKS.

YES! AND WE REALLY EARNED IT!

WELCOME TO...THE TIMS!

THE TIMS

The Tims

CAZENOVE & WILLIAM

ON THIS FESTIVAL DAY, ALL THE YOUNG GIRLS OF THE COUNTRY WERE HASTENING TO *THE CASTLE OF BEAUTIFUL LADIES*...

...FOR THE YOUNG AND CHARMING KING WAS SEEKING A WIFE.

LADY DUCTAPE, LADY INCHARGE, AND LADY GRABBY-HANDZ.

LADY NAT, I DON'T SEE PRINCESS MAUREEN.

UM, WELL, ACTUALLY...

KABOOM

?

YOU DIDN'T START WITHOUT ME, DID YOU?

DON'T EVEN THINK ABOUT MARRYING ONE OF THOSE HOMELY WENCHES!

ƎGAHƐ...

UM, MAUREEN, PROTOCOL!

I DON'T NEED A *PRO* TO CALL!

IT'S NO FUN PLAYING FAIRY TALES WITH YOU, MAUREEN.

YOU'RE JUST JEALOUS!

COME ON-- YOU'RE MY HUBBY AND THAT'S FINAL!

CAZENOVE & WILLIAM

75

JOGGING WITH MY SISTER IS REALLY *MISSION IMPOSSIBLE*.

WENDY, WENDYY... LOOK AT THIS...

OH, NO...IT'S STARTING AGAIN! *~RAAAAHHH...~*

IT'S JUST LIKE THE ONE FROM YESTERDAY, REMEMBER?!

WE'RE NOT GOING TO STOP EVERY FIVE MINUTES TO ADMIRE PEBBLES.

C'MON, GET YOUR REAR IN GEAR.

HOP TO IT!

WAIT. THE ONE OVER THERE IS SUPER-CUTE!

HERE'S ANOTHER CUTE ONE.

OOH! I'VE NEVER SEEN SUCH A PRETTY STONE.

WOW! THESE PEBBLES *ROCK!*

IN FACT, JOGGING WITH MAUREEN CAN BE HAZARDOUS TO YOUR HEALTH.

CAZENOVE & WILLIAM

ZOO MINIATURE ANIMALS

WOW! THEY ARE *SO* CUTE!

DID YOU SEE THAT? I'VE NEVER SEEN SUCH A SMALL COW.

NEITHER HAVE I!

IT'S *INSANE* HOW TEENY-TINY THEY ARE.

LOOK OVER HERE...MINI ELEPHANTS.

THOSE ARE SAMPLES...

IF YOU LIKE THEM, YOU CAN GET A REAL ONE LATER!

THE MINI-PIGS ARE TO SQUEE FOR!

AND THERE'S A MINI-GIRAFFE, AND MINI-ZEBRAS... HEE HEE...

HUGELY CUTE!

LOOK, DADDY, MAUREEN IS A GIANT HERE.

OOH... THEY EVEN HAVE HORSIES MY SIZE!

I COULD EAT THEM UP!

CAN WE GET ONE?

PLEASE, PLEASE SAY YES...

WE'LL TAKE CARE OF IT.

YOU MUST BE JOKING. THEY'RE STILL TOO BIG FOR OUR HOUSE!

SAY, MISTER, COULD YOU MAKE THEM EVEN TINIER?

LIKE EENSY-TEENSY-WEENSY?

VISITORS EXIT

CAZENOVE & WILLIAM

77

PLAYING GAMES WITH MY SISTER IS A REAL PAIN.

SHE NEVER GETS ANYTHING RIGHT.

IN A TRIVIA GAME, SHE MESSES UP THE QUESTIONS.

WHO SAID, UM, HAKU...AKU... KUNA...KUNAMA... MATA...TA?

SHOULD WE SKIP THIS ONE?

YEP!

FOR PICTURE GAMES, SHE CAN'T DRAW A CLUE THAT MAKES SENSE.

SO HERE'S TARZAN IN THE TREES.

A GIRL... AND A DANCING MONKEY.

SO THE ANSWER IS...

"THE CHEETAH GIRLS"!

IF THE GAME INVOLVES MONEY, SHE GOES TOTALLY NUTS.

I'LL TAKE ALL THE PINK ONES...

THEY'RE SO SO PRETTY!

OKAY. LOL. I'LL TAKE $50,000 OF THE UGLY YELLOW ONES.

WHEN A GAME INVOLVES DICE, SHE KEEPS ROLLING THEM UNDER THE FURNITURE.

DOUBLE SIXES!

I SAW IT, I SWEAR!

SINCE SHE NEVER UNDERSTANDS ANYTHING, SHE'S ALWAYS LOST...

...SO, OF COURSE SHE WHINES!

BUT THERE'S STILL ONE GAME SHE ALWAYS WINS!

HA! HA! I'M HIDING AND YOU'LL NEVER FIND ME!

CAZENOVE & WILLIAM

HEY! GET AWAY FROM THERE.

WHAT HAVE YOU FOUND, VIX?

PEYEW! THAT'S DISGUSTING!

NAUGHTY DOGGIE! PUT THAT DOWN!

LET GO OF THE BONE, VIX. I MEAN IT!

THIS ISN'T A GAME.

DROP IT! IT'S GROSS!

AT LAST!

IT JUST TAKES A FIRM HAND.

YOU HAVE TO STAND YOUR GROUND.

DON'T WORRY, WENDY, I'LL GET YOUR NINTENDOX BACK.

I'M USED TO IT.

CAZENOVE & WILLIAM

NO, NO, AND NO! I'M NOT LENDING YOU ONE OF MY FRIENDS!

BUT, WENDYYY... YOU HAVE SO MANY, AND MINE HAVE ALL LEFT ON VACATION...

THAT'S NOT MY PROBLEM.

ALL I NEED IS SAMMIE.

SAMMIE? YOU TWO WOULDN'T GET ALONG. SHE ALWAYS WANTS TO BE RIGHT-- JUST LIKE YOU.

WHAT ABOUT MEGAN? I REALLY LIKE HER.

MEGAN IS WORSE THAN SAMMIE...

...SHE'S CAN'T BEAR TO LOSE, SO SHE ALWAYS CHEATS.

WELL, OKAY. NOT MEGAN.

YOU SEE, NONE OF MY FRIENDS WOULD BE RIGHT FOR YOU.

GO PLAY WITH YOUR DOLLS.

BUT YOU MUST HAVE ONE WHO--

WHAT ABOUT AUDREY? LET ME BORROW HER.

AUDREY?!

SHE'S SO BOY-CRAZY THAT SHE WON'T TALK ABOUT ANYTHING ELSE. BORING!

HEY! WAAAIIIIT! LET ME EXPLAIN! I WAS ONLY SAYING THOSE THINGS SO...

WELL, YOU CAN FORGET ABOUT BORROWING A DOLL FROM ME TO PLAY WITH!

CAZENOVE & WILLIAM

WHAT KIND OF CAKE SHOULD WE MAKE FOR DADDY'S BIRTHDAY?

HERE, I FOUND A COOKBOOK.

LOOK AT ALL THESE RECIPES! TONS OF THEM.

THIS ONE LOOKS NICE. *BAKED... ELASTIC?*

NEVER MIND. IT'S LAME.

OR WE COULD MAKE A PIE INSTEAD.

THERE'S NO SUCH THING AS *BIRTHDAY PIE.* IT HAS TO BE CAKE.

I KNOW! WE COULD MAKE PANCAKES-- HE LOVES 'EM!

YOU'RE NUTS! I DON'T FEEL LIKE CLEANING THE KITCHEN FROM FLOOR TO CEILING.

MARBLE CAKE?

STRAWBERRY SHORTCAKE?

TIRAMISU?

DARK CHOCOLATE PUDDING?

MEH. NAH.

I GOT IT!

SUPER! HE WILL LOVE IT!

FER SHER! IT'S MEGA-NUMMY

COME ON, STIR!

HMM...DARK CHOCOLATE, CHORIZO, EGG NOODLES, CHOPPED STEAK, SPONGE CAKE, GUMMY FRUIT...

WE MADE SURE TO INCLUDE ALL YOUR FAVORITES.

GUARANTEED!

CAZENOVE & WILLIAM

GET UP, WENDY!...THEY'RE STARTING!

ZAK ET FRON

GAH ?!

JUST ONCE YOU'D THINK THEY MIGHT SLEEP IN...

C'MON, WE CAN SEE BETTER FROM MY ROOM.

MOM AND DAD THINK WE'RE STILL ASLEEP. HEE HEE!

LOL! THEY ARE SO NAÏVE.

WENDY, SHOULDN'T WE TELL THEM WE DON'T BELIEVE IN THE EASTER BUNNY ANYMORE?

NO WAY!

ARE YOU AFRAID THEY WOULDN'T BUY US ANY CANDY?

THE TREATS THEY HIDE AREN'T ALL THAT GREAT.

TRUE, BUT HAVE YOU SEEN HOW THEIR EYES LIGHT UP WHEN WE FIND THEM?

WE CAN'T SPOIL THEIR FUN.

GIRLS! THE EASTER BUNNY CAME!

NEXT YEAR WE 'FESS UP ABOUT THE EASTER BUNNY!

FOR SURE!

CAZENOVE & WILLIAM

82

MAUREEN, I WANT TO TEST YOUR SUPER-POWERS.

IF YOU WANT TO.

FIRST, TRY TO BEND THIS BAR FOR ME.

the AMAZING TARANTULA

EASY-PEASY! WHAT WAS IT MADE OF... GRANOLA

NNNNN

AMAZING TARANT

SARGEANT BONK

NOPE! TEMPERED STEEL.

YOU SHOULD FIND THIS MORE DIFFICULT— IT'S ADAMANTIUM.

LIKE IN WOLVERINE'S SKELETON?

HEE HEE. THIS DOODAD IS AS SOFT AS BUTTER.

?!

SKREE

SARGEANT BONK

OKAY! DO YOUR WORST. TRY TO BREAK THIS LITTLE BAR.

ARE YOU TRYING TO INSULT MY SUPER-POWERS?

?!

M

JUST LOOK... IT'S...

NO WORRIES...

≥UNGHHH!

IMPOSSIBLE!... THIS STUFF IS INDESTRUCTIBLE.

LIKE THE LOCK ON MY DIARY?

IT'S NOT FAIRRR!

My Diary Wendy

CAZENOVE & WILLIAM

83

CAZENOVE & WILLIAM

WENDY...

DID YOU KNOW YOU LEFT YOUR DIARY LYING AROUND?

THAT'S *PRIVATE!*

HANDS OFF!

WELL, KEEP IT IN YOUR ROOM, THEN.

♪ TRA LA LA ♪

CHOMP

YESSS!

CLICK

AH-HEM.

THANKS, SIS!

I LOST MY KEY...

...AND I KNEW YOU COULDN'T RESIST OPENING IT. YOU CAN BE SO PREDICTABLE.

CAZENOVE & WILLIAM

CAZENOVE & WILLIAM

STEP RIGHT UP, LADIES AND GENTLEMEN, AND TAKE YOUR SEATS FOR FIVE MINUTES OF TERROR!

THE GHOST TRAIN

SCARY!

CREEPY!

THE HORROR!

IF THEY HATE IT SO MUCH, WHY DO THEY DO IT?

IT HELPS THEM PREPARE...

...FOR THEIR MATH QUIZZES.

CAZENOVE & WILLIAM

SEE YOU TONIGHT. BYE!

LATER!

OKAY, I'M REALLY GOING THIS TIME.

TAP TAP

DID THE BUS COME EARLY *AGAIN?*

HOW DO THEY EXPECT US TO CATCH IT?

88

CAZENOVE & WILLIAM

HEY, MISTER, WHAT'S THIS RUSTY DOOHICKEY?

HUH?

LET'S SEE IF YOU CAN GUESS WHAT IT'S FOR!

UM...

STYLING YOUR HAIR?

HA, HA. NICE TRY.

IT'S FOR USE IN THE *KITCHEN*.

YOU PUT A POTATO ON THIS PRONG, AND WHEN YOU TURN THE HANDLE, THE PEELER TAKES ALL THE SKIN OFF.

WOW!

NOW I SEE! HOW CLEVER!

DOES IT ONLY WORK ON POTATOES?

OH, NO. YOU CAN PEEL LOTS OF THINGS, LIKE APPLES AND ZUCCHINI.

YOU CAN HAVE IT FOR $5.

WE'LL TAKE IT!

CAN YOU GIFT-WRAP IT?

SINCE WE BROKE YOUR FOOD PROCESSOR, WE THOUGHT WE SHOULD REPLACE IT.

AND YOU DON'T EVEN HAVE TO PLUG IT IN!

CAZENOVE & WILLIAM

THE MONSTER IS LOOSE, SUPER M!

HE'LL DESTROY THE WHOLE CITY!

BUT I *WON'T* LET HIM MUSS UP MY HAIR!

SINCE HE LIKES TO INHALE THINGS, LET'S GIVE HIM A LITTLE PRESENT.

THE WATER TOWER! GREAT IDEA, SUPER W!

HI-YAAH!

THIS SHOULD DO IT...ON THREE!

CRACK

ONE... TWO...

...THREE!

LOVE THAT FACE HE'S MAKING!

GASP!

LET'S GET OUT OF HERE BEFORE HE BARFS ON US! LOL!

BETTER NOT BOTHER THE *SUPER SISTERS!*

⸘AAARGH!‽ WHAT ON EARTH DID YOU DO TO THE VACUUM CLEANER?

IT WON'T HURT ANYONE EVER AGAIN!

DON'T FORGET TO GIVE ME BACK THE WATER TOWER WHEN YOU GET IT OUT, DADDY.

CAZENOVE & WILLIAM

WE HAVE LOTS OF ACTIVITIES.

YEAH! WE'RE OVER-BOOKED.

AFTER DANCE LESSONS, I GO HORSEBACK RIDING FOR TWO HOURS...

PLUS I STUDY FENCING, LIKE ZORRO.

YOU MUST LEARN TO MAKE A "Z" WITH YOUR BLADE!

THEN I GO TO VIDEO CLUB. WE'RE MAKING A PIRATE MOVIE.

I'M REALLY GOOD AT PIRATING MOVIES.

LOL!

HA HA!

HEY! NO DOWNLOADING!

MAUREEN DOES SWIMMING AND JUDO.

I DIDN'T HAVE TIME TO CHANGE!

MOM AND DAD REALIZED WE WERE DOING TOO MUCH.

YOU HAVE TO CUT DOWN...CHOOSE SOMETHING TO GIVE UP.

WE WANT TO GIVE UP *SCHOOL*!

WRITE 100 TIMES: "SCHOOL IS THE KEY TO SUCCESS."

THEY SAY WE'RE DOING TOO MUCH... AND THEN THEY GIVE US MORE TO DO!

GO FIGURE...

CAZENOVE & WILLIAM

I GOT IT!

IT'S BLUE-INDIGO.

NO, I MEANT GRASS GREEN.

HERE WE GO AGAIN.

OR CANDY PINK.

BUTTER YELLOW?

MUSTARD YELLOW?

GRAY-VIOLET?

NOW SHE'S PLAYING TWENTY QUESTIONS...

ENOUGH ALREADY! I'M FED UP, MAUREEN!

TIME TO GIVE UP.

IN YOUR DREAMS!

REMEMBER WHAT I TOLD YOU WHEN WE WERE LITTLE?!

HOW COULD I FORGET?

OKAY, THIS CAN'T GO ON ALL NIGHT...DO YOU GIVE UP?

NO! NEVER! I'LL NEVER GIVE UP!

I'LL FIND THE ANSWER, EVEN IF IT TAKES YEARS!

Riddle

What color was George Washington's white horse?

HERE WE GO!

CAZENOVE & WILLIAM

WATCH OUT FOR PAPERCUTZ

Welcome to the second-in-a-series of squabbling sibling stories—THE SISTERS graphic novel, by Christophe Cazenove and William Maury, from Papercutz—those family-friendly folks dedicated to publishing great graphic novels for all ages. I'm Jim Salicrup, the Editor-in-Chief and big brother, and I'm here to take you behind-the-scenes at Papercutz…

While the majority of the fans for THE SISTERS may in fact be female, I'm also a fan of THE SISTERS and I'm a guy. And it's not just because the artwork by William Maury is so awesome or the clever writing by Christophe Cazenove is so funny, although I certainly enjoy well-written and beautifully drawn graphic novels. No, it's because I simply like Wendy and Maureen, the stars of this super-fun series, and their relationship to each other. As I mentioned, I'm an older brother. I still remember that day when I was just three years old and my parents came home with my baby brother—William Salicrup (He's so tired of hearing this story!). Months earlier my parents had asked if I wanted a little brother, and I happily agreed. But I didn't realize he'd be a baby! I thought they'd get me a brother who was already old enough for me to play with. But what did I know? I was only three years old at the time and didn't fully understand how these kinds of things worked.

I also remember my mom teasing me, saying that I was like a little old man because when we'd go to the playground, rather than run around and play, I preferred to sit with her. Well, after my brother came along, her hands were full chasing him around. He was like a Tasmanian Devil—like the one in the Warner Bros. cartoons. He was a bundle of energy, while I tended to just sit there. Fortunately, as Editor-in-Chief of Papercutz, all I have to do is sit at my desk and work. Who knew I was training to be graphic novel editor at such an early age?

Not only did my little brother keep my mom busy, he kept me busy as well. He simply demanded attention all of the time. And that's why I can relate to Wendy and how she has to deal with her younger sister Maureen. Sure they're girls, but aside from their specific interests they weren't all that different from how my brother and I acted toward each other when we were young.

But no matter how crazy I might think my childhood was, it's nothing compared to that of Lincoln Loud's! Lincoln doesn't have a little brother, or even a bigger brother—he has ten sisters: Lori (the oldest), Leni (the beauty), Luna (the rock star), Luan (the jokester), Lynn (the sport), Lucy (the emo), Lisa (the genius), Lily (the poop machine), and Lola and Lana (the twins). If they sound familiar, that's because they're the stars of the hit new Nickelodeon series *The Loud House*, created by Chris Savino. And they're also starring in an all-new graphic novel series from Papercutz! Not only will you find them in THE LOUD HOUSE graphic novels, but they'll be popping up, along with other super-stars such as *Sanjay and Craig*, *Breadwinners*, *Harvey Beaks*, and *Pig Goat Banana Cricket*, in the pages of NICKELODEON PANDEMONIUM yet another super-cool series from Papercutz.

And speaking of cool graphic novel series from Papercutz, check out the preview pages from DANCE CLASS #8 "Snow White and the Seven Dwarves." Friends and fellow dance students Julie, Alia, and Lucie are the stars of DANCE CLASS, but we do sometimes get a peek at the relationship between Julie and her younger sister Capucine. If you look real closely at parts of this graphic novel, you'll discover that Wendy and Maureen are obviously DANCE CLASS fans too!

And if THE LOUD HOUSE, NICKELODEON PANDEMONIUM, and DANCE CLASS series aren't enough to satisfy your need for great graphic novels until THE SISTERS #3 "Honestly, I Love My Sister" comes along, then look at what else we have to offer at papercutz.com. You'll be glad you did!

Thanks,

Jim

STAY IN TOUCH!

EMAIL: salicrup@papercutz.com
WEB: www.papercutz.com
TWITTER: @papercutzgn
FACEBOOK: PAPERCUTZGRAPHICNOVELS
REGULAR MAIL: Papercutz, 160 Broadway, Suite 700,
                East Wing, New York, NY 10038

Copyright © 2016 Viacom International Inc. All Rights Reserved. Nickelodeon, Sanjay and Craig, The Loud House, Harvey Beaks, Pig Goat Banana Cricket and all related titles, logos and characters are trademarks of Viacom International Inc.

EVERYTHING'S OKAY. OUR SNOW WHITE LOOKS LIKE SHE'LL BE ALL RIGHT!

LUCKILY I DIDN'T HAVE TO KISS HER!

BUT NOW THAT I THINK ABOUT IT, MARY, WHO'LL PLAY THE ROLE OF THE SEVEN DWARVES?

THE CHILDREN FROM THE DANCE SCHOOL! MISS ANNE WENT TO GET THEM.

THUMP THUMP THUMP

AND IN FACT, I HEAR THEM COMING!

HELLO, EVERYONE!

WE'RE HERE!

WHEN DO WE START?

THUMP

THUMP

THIS IS SO COOL, JULIE! I GET TO DANCE WITH MY BIG SISTER!

YES, CAPUCINE!

ARE YOU SNOW WHITE?

WE'LL BE TOGETHER ALL THE TIME AT REHEARSAL THEN?

IT'LL BE FUN!

GET AWAY, YOU DORKS!

I NEED AIR!

IT'S OFF TO A BAD START! APPARENTLY, SNOW WHITE CAN'T STAND THE SEVEN DWARVES!

© 2013 BAMBOO EDITION

DID YOU SEE THE REHEARSAL SCHEDULE? WE DON'T HAVE MUCH TIME BEFORE THE DAY OF THE SHOW.

SO, STARTING FROM NOW, I HAVE TO TRY TO PUT MYSELF IN THE WICKED QUEEN'S CHARACTER!

THAT'LL BE HARD!

WHY DO YOU SAY THAT?

BECAUSE YOU'RE ALWAYS NICE, JULIE! LOOK! YOU'RE CARRYING YOUR LITTLE SISTER'S BAG WITHOUT HER HAVING TO ASK YOU!

THAT'S TRUE! YOU'RE RIGHT, LUCIE.

HERE, CAPUCINE! AFTER ALL, YOU'RE BIG ENOUGH TO CARRY IT YOURSELF!

!

YOU KNOW, JULIE, MAYBE YOU DON'T NEED TO START PLAYING THE EVIL QUEEN STARTING TONIGHT. I THINK IT'D BE BETTER TOMORROW.

OH, WHY?

WELL, I WAS COUNTING ON YOU TO HELP ME DO MY MATH HOMEWORK!

THAT'S OKAY, ALIA! LET'S DO IT RIGHT NOW, IF YOU LIKE.

COOL! SINCE YOU'RE NICE AGAIN, YOU CAN TAKE MY BAG BACK!

!

Don't Miss DANCE CLASS #8 "Snow White and the Seven Dwarves"
Available Now at Booksellers Everywhere!